THE MYSTERY OF COTTAGE COVE

The Mystery of Cottage Cove

Written by Aleda Renken
Art by Michael Norman

A Haley Adventure Book

Publishing House
St. Louis

Concordia Publishing House, St. Louis, Missouri

Copyright © 1975 by Concordia Publishing House

MANUFACTURED IN THE UNITED STATES OF AMERICA

Library of Congress Cataloging in Publication Data

Renken, Aleda.
    The Mystery of Cottage Cove.

    (A Haley adventure book)
    SUMMARY: For their vacation the Haley family
knowingly rents a haunted place at the lake, quite
convinced a ghost won't bother them.
    [1. Mystery and detective stories] I. Norman,
Michael. II. Title.
PZ7.R289My   [Fic]   75-5578
ISBN 0-570-07232-8

2 3 4 5 6 7 8 9 10 11   DB   90 89 88 87 86 85 84 83 82 81

CHAPTER 1

Pat sat by the telephone in the front hall watching the big hall clock and nervously waiting for the telephone to ring. She was alone in the house. Her mother and youngest brother had gone shopping with neighbor boy Sam's granny. Pat could have gone with them, but the last thing her oldest brother Kurt had said before he, her brother Jeff, and Sam had left was, "So far Red hasn't gotten a shortstop for our team, so we'll probably call on you. How fast can you run a mile and a half?"

"Try me! I'll be there before you can breathe twice." Pat loved to play baseball. She *knew* she was a very good shortstop. She was fast and sure, her reflexes as good as those of any boy around.

"He's going to try to get Fat Simmons," Jeff said doubtfully. He didn't want Pat to be disappointed.

"But I'm a much better shortstop."

"Of course you are," Sam agreed.

"But the trouble is, you're not a boy, and this is for boys," Kurt reminded her.

"Oh, of course! Don't let me forget that!"

Pat said icily. "I can run faster than that fat slob, I can throw better, and I'm a lot smarter; but since Fat is a boy and I'm just a girl, he gets all the breaks."

"There's nothing we can do about that," Kurt said as he picked up his glove and bat. "Come on guys, let's go."

"If Fat isn't there, I'll call you from Higgin's house," Jeff said; but he looked and sounded as if he didn't have much hope.

The phone didn't ring, and at last Pat had to face the fact that she was not going to be called. Okay, let that dumb fat boy miss a few hits, let him make error after error. It serves him right. She wished with all her might that her brothers' team would lose 50 to 0.

She pitched her ball glove at the front screen door and almost hit her father in the face as he came in.

"Are we having a temper tantrum?" he asked.

"Dad, I'm sorry! I was mad because I didn't get to play baseball with the boys. They got Fat instead of me."

Mr. Haley headed for the kitchen.

"And do you know why?" Pat followed her father.

"Because he's a boy and you're a girl." Mr. Haley got out a jug of orange juice and poured himself a glass. "Where's your mother?"

"She went shopping with Granny. Donnie went with them."

"I'll leave her a note." Mr. Haley got out a pen and started to write on the bulletin board. "Now, run upstairs and change from those jeans into a dress, and you'll soon forget you were rejected as a shortstop just because you're a girl."

Pat put on her favorite green print and her white sandals. She combed her hair and tied it back with a ribbon to match her dress.

Her father was waiting at the bottom of the steps. "Now, that's what I call a good-looking date," he said, smiling. "Come on, let's go; and I'll tell you what we're going to do.

Pat got in the front seat and fastened her seat belt. They were out on the highway before her father explained.

"I have to appraise some property at the lake, and after I've done that, you and I are going to look for a good place to have a 2-week vacation for all of us — Granny and Sam too."

Pat sat up straight, "Oh, Dad, that sounds wonderful! Does Mom know?"

"No, because I didn't know myself until today. My boss said there's a slack period now and I deserve a vacation. So, we'll just pick out a place all by ourselves and surprise the family."

"Sam and Granny too? You know Granny

won't leave her house and chickens for 2 weeks."

"She will if she can have someone to take care of all her things. I think her two brothers, Uncle Henry and Uncle Hugo, can do something for her. She's always doing something for them. Besides, I'll pay them, and they can look in at our house and cut the grass."

Pat gave a happy little bounce. "Oh, it will be fun! We can swim and ski and fish. But we'll have to rent two cottages, Dad."

We'll find something," her father promised.

While her father was looking over some property, Pat sat in the car and planned all the things they could do. The Haley family had never taken a vacation with Granny and Sam. At last Mr. Haley came out of the real estate office. "We're all set now," he smiled. "And we don't have to hurry. I wrote your mother not to expect us home for dinner because we can eat on the way. Would you like that?"

"I'd love it!" Pat cried. Let those boys get Fat to fumble around with the ball. She would rather be with her father picking out a vacation spot than throwing out a fast runner at first base. Besides it was a beautiful day, the kind of day when a person expected something wonderful to happen. A few cloud puffs raced across the blue sky and reflected on the sparkling water. It was going to be great to live on the lake for 2 weeks.

But after they had made three stops at resorts and found they were all booked up for the month, Pat and her father began to get uneasy.

"Oh, I do hope we don't have to go back without finding a place," worried Pat.

"We won't," soothed her father." "The place we're going to now is one the real estate agent told me about. It's called Cottage Cove and it's at a reasonable price. We just might find them vacant for next week. The agent said she seldom had renters — although I don't know why."

He peered at a small wooden sign at a crossroad. "We've got to find Lake Road 5-66, Dogwood Lane."

"This is it. Oh, look, Dad, there are wild flowers everywhere! Too bad wild flowers won't last when picked; I'd love to take some to Mom."

"Wild flowers are most beautiful in the wild. Let's hope your mother can see them for herself next week."

The car twisted and turned on the little dirt road that wound so prettily under tall oaks. At last, right beside the road they saw a white frame house that looked as if it had been closed for the season. The shades were all drawn and there wasn't a sign of anyone around.

"This must be it," Mr. Haley said as he stopped the car.

"Oh, Dad, look down the hill!" Pat cried. See? There are three cottages all made of rock. Aren't they darling?"

"Pat jumped up out of the car and looked down the hill. "There are rock walls with vines and flowers. And the cottages are all closed up! Oh, I do hope someone's around to talk to us."

A man with a string of fish came around the bend of the road. He nodded and smiled when Mr. Haley greeted him.

"Do you know if someone's at home here?"

"Elizabeth Sweeny owns it, and I'm sure she's home. She hardly ever goes anyplace anymore."

"You live there?" Mr. Haley pointed to a house set far back among the trees across the road.

"Yep, that's my place. I got a couple of cottages too, but I can't get any renters. People want to be right smack on the water now, and we have nothing but a steep path to the lake."

The man was short but had powerful arms and shoulders. A dark mass of straggly hair poked out from under his old fishing hat, and his eyes were friendly.

"Nice catch of fish," Mr. Haley said.

"Most times it's good fishing there on

10

Elizabeth's dock. But I don't fish there 'cause Elizabeth's kind of funny that way, ever since I told her I'd like to buy her place. Those cottages are dandies. Her man built—"

A sudden shrill whistle from the woods and a crackling of leaves interrupted him, and someone stepped out of the bushes and stopped short when he saw Mr. Haley and Pat. In an instant he dived back out of sight, but not before Pat noticed that he was a boy with a cap pulled down over his ears and a sullen, angry look on his face.

Mr. Haley shrugged and said, "Well, we'd better go see her. We'd like to rent the place for a couple of weeks."

The man gave a sheepish grin and nodded toward the bushes where the boy had disappeared. "Kind of bashful. I'm sure you can rent it. If you do, I'll be seeing you. My name's Abbett."

"Thanks, Mr. Abbett. Oh, here's Mrs. Sweeny now."

A woman stepped out of the white frame house and waited on the porch. Her hair was flaming red and many deeply grooved wrinkles lined her face. She just missed being pretty by a little bit, Pat thought, partly because she wore two blotches of bright rouge on her cheekbones and partly because her lipstick made her mouth a shape it wasn't supposed to be.

"I'm Robert Haley, and this is my daughter, Patricia. We were told of your place, and we wondered if your cottages were booked for the next 2 weeks?"

Mrs. Sweeny smiled at Pat, but her eyes were sad.

"No, no, they aren't taken. I have three cottages. The biggest has two bedrooms. The other two only one."

"They're very pretty," said Mr. Haley. "We'd need all three for my bunch. What would the rental of them be for about 2 weeks?"

Pat turned and ran down the rock steps, past the cottages, and then down another flight of steps to the dock below. The water looked very deep, a lovely blue green. There were three boats tied to the dock. One had a fairly large motor – surely large enough to take them skiing. The cove was quiet. Across it stood no resorts, just dogwood and scrub oaks climbing the hill. But Pat could look far out to the main channel, and there she saw sailboats and a big houseboat.

She loved it all. Yes, they *would* have fun. With a little practice she'd soon be skiing as well as the boys. And Donnie, her smallest brother, could learn too. Maybe even her mother would try.

She looked across at the next lot, which must belong to the man named Abbett. Parts of a rough path led up to the road, and what was left of the dock stood partly in water. The boat tied to it looked as if it was half full of water. No wonder he got no renters, Pat thought.

She started up the steps but paused when she saw through the bushes and trees an old leaning shed on Mr. Abbett's side of the property. It wasn't the half-torn-down shed that interested her but the person leaning back against one of the walls.

Pat knew that the shed couldn't be seen from where her father and Mrs. Sweeny were standing. But this person — maybe the same boy who dived into the bushes on top of the hill — stood there, listening. Pat wondered what her father and Mrs. Sweeny were talking about. Yes, she was sure it was the same boy, because he had that tan cap pulled low, shading half his face.

At last she ran up the steps and Mr. Haley turned to her.

"How do you like it, Pat?" he asked.

"I love it."

"Don't you want to go and look at the cottages?" Mrs. Sweeny took a bunch of keys out of her pocket.

So the three of them went down and looked at the spotless cabins. Mr. Haley got more enthusiastic by the minute.

13

"We'll take them! We'll be here next week, unless I call you."

"I don't—my phone doesn't work. Drop me a card if you aren't coming." Mrs. Sweeny spoke slowly, as if it took a lot of effort to say each word.

"I'm sure the rest of the family will want to come. So we'll be here."

"I—I think I should tell you one thing before you make up your mind." Mrs. Sweeny's chin trembled and Pat tried not to look at her.

Mr. Haley waited patiently, but his eyes gleamed when he looked at the three cottages, the big fireplace on the patio, and the three boats tied to the dock.

"I know people in town say my place is haunted. No—wait please, until I finish. You see, my husband built this place. I helped him. We were going to have a celebration after he fitted the last rock in the wall over there."

They glanced at the wall—it was easier than looking at Mrs. Sweeny's sad face.

"But he had a heart attack the day he put down the last rock. He died right there by the wall." She stared at it, a tear rolling over the rouge and onto her chin.

"I'm sorry," Mr. Haley said.

Pat would have liked to touch her hand, pat her arm, anything that might help, but she

15

didn't think she really knew her well enough. And some people didn't like to be touched.

"There was a bunch of women who rented the place this spring," continued Mrs. Sweeny. "They intended staying a week, but the first night three of them said they saw a ghost carrying a rock. They pulled out the next day. I gave their money back."

"Mrs. Sweeny, I don't think there's one in our party that would hesitate to rent this attractive place," said Mr. Haley firmly. "You don't think anyone would be afraid, do you, Pat?

"No, I don't. We don't believe in ghosts."

"I don't know how that story got around so fast," sighed Mrs. Sweeny, but everyone in town knew it, and I haven't had renters since."

"Well, we'll tell a different story in the village when we're here. See you next week. Come on, Pat." Mr. Haley started toward the car. Pat smiled at Mrs. Sweeny and followed him.

"She's nice, but she's so sad." Pat looked back as they pulled away. "My, but she must be scared."

"Why do you say that?" Mr. Haley drove slowly through the curves and turns.

"Because her whole house is shut up so tight and because just now she locked the screen door behind her and I guess the other door too."

"I suppose you do get to feeling that way when you're alone all the time. Pat, don't you think the family and Granny and Sam will love this place?"

"They will, Dad, and I do too. Now, I'm getting hungry." Pat settled back in the seat, thinking how much fun it was going to be to tell the family.

CHAPTER 2

Pat stood back, surveying the pile of things she had stacked to take along on vacation. It looked like an awfully big stack, but she felt she needed every bit of it. She heard her father's footsteps on the stairs, and her mother called from the hall below.

"Hope you have everything ready! Dad's coming to get it and put it in a box in the station wagon."

He came to the doorway of Pat's room, and she held her breath.

"You wouldn't believe it!" he shouted to Mrs. Haley. "These kids have packed enough junk to take us to Africa and back. Will you please come up and help them remove two-thirds? Why are you boys taking all that baseball stuff? There's no place to play ball."

"Just thought we could do a little batting practice," Jeff whispered.

"Anyway, *I* didn't take many clothes," Donnie said proudly.

"No, you didn't take enough," replied his father. "But how about those packages of raisins, dry cereal, cookies, two cold hot dogs, and a peanut-butter sandwich?"

"I thought we might want them to eat on the way down."

"It's less than a 3-hour drive. You won't starve in that time," laughed Kurt. "Besides, a little starving would be good for you."

Mrs. Haley came upstairs. "You go on down, dear. They can bring their things down as soon as I sort them. They haven't gone away often enough to learn what to take."

Pat was figuring what she should remove from her stack of clothes when her mother came in.

"You don't need 10 pairs of shorts, Pat. Granny and I will have to go to the laundromat at least two or three times anyway."

Mr. Haley had come upstairs again and was in the boys' room. "I didn't know I had sons who were clothes horses. Put those good shoes back. All you need is tennis shoes. Remember, we have eight people and a dog. That's a lot, even for our big station wagon. We want to take some food—I'm sure you don't want that left behind."

"I'll put your things in my suitcase, Pat," Mrs. Haley offered. "Just be sure you've got your swimsuit."

Pat glanced out the window. "Dad, here comes Uncle Hugo!" she called.

Mr. Haley ran down the steps, and the boys heaved a sigh of relief.

"What makes him get so excited whenever we go anyplace?" Kurt asked.

"Is Uncle Hugo the one who is going to cut our grass and stuff?" Donnie looked out the window too.

"I guess so." Kurt gathered up his bundle of clothes.

"Oh, boy, I'll bet he won't clip the hedges right!" gloated Donnie. "Won't Dad be mad when we get home and everything looks sloppy?" He gleefully followed Kurt downstairs.

"Leave room for the food Granny is going to bring, dear," Mrs. Haley called from the kitchen.

And then there was no more room. They had to take everything out and repack it, and Mr. Haley was gritting his teeth, trying to be patient.

"Leave the dumb dog at home," Kurt suggested.

"I can't leave my dog here!" wailed Donnie. "Mom, did you hear him? He–"

"Shhhhh." Mrs. Haley glanced at her husband. "Boys, go upstairs and be sure that all the windows are closed. Then I suppose we can leave."

While the boys were gone, Poochie got

bored with the whole thing and went off to chase a squirrel.

"I've half a mind to leave him here," Mr. Haley said sternly. He was already behind the wheel.

"No, no, we can't!" Donnie cried. "Jeff please help me find him!"

They finally found Poochie barking at a turtle in the creek. He was standing in the water up to his belly.

"We've *got* to dry him. He can't get in the car sopping wet. Get a towel or rag, Donnie. Dad's about to blow a gasket," Jeff warned.

Finally they had Poochie at the back of the station wagon. He took one look at the tiny space they'd left him and refused to budge.

"Well?" Mr. Haley called from the front seat.

"Get in the back of the wagon and pull as hard as you can. I'll push," Jeff whispered.

Poochie thought it was a new game and sat firmly on the ground. Kurt looked back, saw the trouble they were in, and took a newspaper from one of the boxes. He got out of the car. One glance at the rolled-up paper and Poochie jumped in. Finally they were ready to go pick up Granny and Sam.

They put Granny's food in the back, but there simply wasn't enough room for a suitcase, so they put it under their feet. Granny was in front with Mr. and Mrs. Haley, and Pat and the four boys were in the back seat. It was fine for Donnie, but the big boys had trouble finding room for their legs. They said nothing, though, and at last the station wagon was on its way. Then Pat began to giggle.

"What's so funny?" Kurt asked.

"You look just like a grasshopper with your face on the top of your knees like that."

Kurt glared at her but said nothing. He knew that the last thing his father could take at that time was a big argument from the back seat.

"I just hope Henry doesn't forget to feed my chickens," Granny worried.

"He won't," replied Sam. "He never forgets feeding time. He'll probably eat five times a day himself with all those goodies you left him."

When they were well on their way, Mr. Haley told Mrs. Sweeny's story about the ghost.

"What kind of ghost would dare to haunt while this gang was there?" Sam laughed.

"She said the people said it was the ghost of her dead husband," Pat explained. "He died carrying the last rock. Three women said they saw it."

"How many times did they see it?" Sam asked.

"Only once. They left the next day, and Mrs. Sweeny gave their money back."

"Gosh, this sounds like a great place," sighed Jeff. "We can swim and ski all day long and at night we can go ghost hunting."

Mr. Haley smiled. "No self-respecting ghost would come around with you three boys there."

"Four," Donnie corrected.

"Come on, Donnie, you're scared already," said Kurt. "You'd go up in smoke if you saw anyone walk across the patio at night."

"I'm tired of the ghost talk," said Mrs. Haley. "Granny, Pat and I have a surprise for you. You've got to promise to use it though."

Granny looked doubtfully at Mrs. Haley. "I've got to promise to use it, or else I won't get it?"

"Right. And you have to decide now, even though we won't give it to you till later."

"I'll take it," said Granny. "As far as I can remember I never got anything I didn't at least try to use."

Pat and her mother looked at each other and smiled.

CHAPTER 3

It was late afternoon when they reached Cottage Cove. And since everyone was starved, they got out the food immediately. As they sat around the big concrete table, they watched the lake turn gold in the rays of the slanting sun.

"Since this is to be a vacation for all of us," Mr. Haley said, "I'm hereby laying down some rules. We'll have teams of two for all dishes and cleanup. Granny and Mother will do most of the cooking, but they'll never have to clean up. Right?"

They all agreed.

"Also, since I know how much both Granny and Mother love sunsets, the big boys and I will take turns taking them out for sunset boat rides. Okay?"

"My goodness!" Granny laughed. "We'll be getting fat and lazy."

"Come on, the sun's going down." Mr. Haley jumped up and ran down the steps to the dock. Granny and Mrs. Haley followed; and soon the motor sounded, and the boat broke the smooth gold of the water.

"Well, thank goodness we used paper

plates for this meal," Pat said as she scraped them and stacked them neatly in the open fireplace. "Let's have a fire and some music tonight. I saw a big stack of wood on the side of each cottage. Donnie, why don't you begin bringing in some logs?"

"If they aren't too heavy."

"If you see the ghost, call us," Kurt teased.

Donnie hesitated and looked around as though he really expected to see a white figure come out of the bushes. When he saw the others laughing, he pushed himself toward a woodpile.

"Don't you tease him about that," Pat scolded. "Can't you remember how you felt when you were that age? I'll bet you weren't so brave and bold then."

"I hope I wasn't as big a coward as Donnie," Kurt said, as he swept the patio.

"I'll bet you were." Pat picked up a big platter with all the used eating utensils on it. She went into the big cottage and dumped them in the sink.

"Tell us the truth, Pat, did Dad just make up that ghost story to get us excited, or is it really true?" Jeff asked, drying five forks at once.

"Mrs. Sweeny told Dad. I heard her. I don't know whether she thinks it's true or not, but she says everyone in the next town

25

seems to have heard it, and so no one comes here anymore—except us."

"That's a shame," Sam said. "That makes me really anxious to find out who that ghost is. I'd like to know who'd be little enough to try and keep renters away from these cottages."

"That's the way I feel too," Pat said, slamming the cup in her sink of suds. "Let's find out if we can."

"That ghost won't come near with us around," boasted Kurt.

"A ghost isn't afraid of *anyone*," Donnie said, dumping two small logs near the fireplace. "I once read—"

"Oh, come on, you hardly can read now," Kurt sneered.

"I remember I read you a story about a ghost, Donnie," soothed Pat. "But, that was only a make-believe story. There are no ghosts."

Donnie wasn't exactly convinced, and he gladly let the boys get the rest of the wood for the fireplace.

Pat was to share one of the small cottages with Granny, Kurt and Sam had the other one, and Jeff and Donnie had the second bedroom in the bigger cottage, where Mr. and Mrs. Haley would stay. Jeff would have liked being with the big boys, but he hardly ever argued any decisions.

"You can spend the evening with us until

bedtime," Sam said, guessing how Jeff felt.

"I might as well. Donnie goes to bed with the birds."

Sam built a big fire in the patio fireplace and they pulled the chairs up around its warmth. The evening breeze was chilly enough to make a fire welcome. It was a beautiful evening too. Far off they could hear the calls of a whippoorwill and other night birds. In the east a fingernail moon climbed the night sky. Then they heard the hum of a motor and saw a bright light on a boat headed toward their cove.

Jeff got out his harmonica and played softly. Donnie crowded in a big chair with Pat, his eyes darting at flickering shadows the fire made. Pat could feel him trembling.

"You cold?" she asked.

"No. I just hope that boat out there is Dad with Mom and Granny."

And then suddenly Mrs. Sweeny appeared, standing near the edge of the flickering firelight. Donnie would have jumped had he not been wedged too tightly in the chair with Pat.

"I didn't mean to scare you," Mrs. Sweeny said in her faraway voice.

No one answered though because they were staring at what Mrs. Sweeny placed on the table. It was a shotgun.

"I brought the gun in case you need it," she said.

"What would we need a gun for?" Sam asked.

"For copperheads. When we built this place my husband and I saw several of them."

Kurt looked at Sam, then cleared his throat. "We're really not too scared of snakes, Ma'am. We live in the country near a creek, so we've seen them lots — and we respect them. But we've found that if you leave them alone, they'll do the same for you."

Mrs. Sweeny looked uncertainly at the boys but did not pick up the gun. "In case of a prowler?" She almost whispered it.

Sam picked up the gun and held it out to her. "I'm sure we won't need it, but we do thank you."

"I don't want you to be afraid." Mrs. Sweeny seemed to be talking to herself. "I hope you won't be afraid."

"I don't know why we should be afraid, Mrs. Sweeny," Pat said gently.

"No, I suppose not. Good night." In a second the darkness had taken her away and they heard a few pebbles roll down the steps.

"She's *weird!*" Kurt said softly. "I don't really think she brought that gun down here because of copperheads."

"I don't either," Sam agreed.

"Then there must be something else she wanted us to protect ourselves from." Jeff said.

"Like what?" Pat asked.

They heard voices from the dock, and soon Granny and Mr. and Mrs. Haley topped the hill.

"It was beautiful, just gorgeous!" Mrs. Haley said, sinking into a chair near the fire.

"This is pretty too," Granny added. "The fire with all the young people around it."

"We had a visitor," said Kurt. "Mrs. Sweeny brought us a gun."

"A gun! What on earth for?" Mr. Haley looked shocked.

"She said for copperheads."

"I'd be a lot more uneasy about a loaded gun than a copperhead," said Mr. Haley. "You kids know better than to run in the woods after dark anyway."

They sang all the songs they knew. Then Mrs. Haley discovered that Donnie had fallen asleep and thought it was time for all of them to go to bed.

"Tie your dog up, Donnie," Mr. Haley said. "If Mother will give you an old rug, we'll put it right here by the yard light, so he can do his watchdog thing."

"He'll bark," Donnie warned sleepily.

Poochie did bark, but not for long. Soon all the lights were out in the cottages, and the dog curled up and went to sleep too.

Pat was awakened by a low deep growl from Poochie, whose rug was under her window. The dog was standing up, his ears straight, his eyes staring at the end of the patio, where the steps went down to the dock.

"It's all right, Pooch," she whispered. "Lie down and go back to sleep." But the dog ignored her, giving another deep growl.

Pat knew that Poochie wasn't the very smartest dog in the world, but she also knew he seldom growled and when he did, he was warning them.

Across the room Granny was snoring peacefully. Pat got up and slipped on tennis shoes. She tiptoed noiselessly out of the bedroom and went outside. Jeff was coming across the patio. He went over to the dog and spoke softly.

"He's trying to warn us of something," Pat whispered.

"Whatever it was, it must be gone because he's ready to get to sleep again."

"Good. I'm not too crazy about sleeping so close to him. I can almost hear him breathe."

"Let's go back to bed. Now, you keep quiet, you bum," Jeff said, giving Poochie another pat.

They had just separated to go back to their cottages when Poochie suddenly sprang up, his hair rising on his shoulders and a deep, angry growl in his throat.

"Something's still here! Only it's over by the wall now!" Pat said.

"You 'fraid to go see?" Jeff asked.

"Of course not."

So they went over to the wall, not daring to get off the patio because they knew that copperheads were night prowlers. There was no sign of anyone, though, and Poochie had settled down again.

"Let's get back to bed," Jeff said, turning to go back to his cottage. Pat hurried back to hers, hoping Granny was still asleep. The steady, soft snoring was still going on, and Pat settled down for the night.

The next morning she awoke to the smell of frying bacon and cooking coffee. Granny's cot was empty, and someone had already set the table. In a few minutes Pat was up and dressed. It was a beautiful day. Poochie was eating and looked as eager as she was to get started on a new day. She ran to the big cottage and yelled from the doorway. "Anything I can do to help?"

"Yes, you may help carry out when we're ready," her mother answered. "The big boys and Dad and Donnie are fishing."

"Pat, come here!" called Jeff. He was trying to roll a rock that was larger than a bowling ball and nearly as round.

31

"Come on, hurry, before someone sees us. It's a wonder they didn't see it when they went fishing," he muttered as Pat joined him.

"Why can't they see it? I hate to get my blouse dirty messing with that rock."

"Just help me get it back in that hole, and I'll explain."

The two of them heaved and pushed and finally lifted the rock and dropped it into a hole, where it fit exactly.

"All right, tell me what it's all about." Pat brushed the dirt off her blouse.

"Did you see how that rock fitted into the hole? Someone had chiseled it out of the wall, the same someone who was around last night when the dog growled. I figure he hid in the woods when we walked over there, and after we were gone he took that rock and put it out on the patio."

"But why?" Pat frowned, staring at the rock in the wall. Just looking at it no one would ever know it had been taken out.

"Think. What was that story you heard Mrs. Sweeny tell Dad?"

"I get it!" Pat cried, her face clearing. "Someone is trying to make us believe it's a ghost moving that rock. You don't think it could be Kurt or Sam playing a trick on us?"

"I thought of that," admitted Jeff. "And that's why I'd rather not say anything yet."

"We're ready for you," called Mrs. Haley. "Jeff, call your father and the boys for breakfast."

Mr. Haley came up, carrying a big string of fish. "Caught them in those rocks by the dock. When you swim, better go more to the right of the dock. Ruth, I want you to try this early morning fishing sometime."

"I'd love to. Why don't you put them back in the water now; then we'll take a picture of you holding them after breakfast. Everyone always takes pictures of their catches."

Pat could hardly take her eyes off the rock in the wall. She almost forgot to eat.

"You missed your mouth for the third time. Look at your eggy blouse!" Kurt laughed.

"She's still asleep." Jeff looked at Pat warningly.

"This afternoon we're going to ski," Mr. Haley announced.

"Goody, goody! I know I can learn, I know it!" Donnie shouted.

"Don't be that sure, bud. Some learn and some never do," Kurt said.

"I'm the kind that learns," Donnie announced.

"And I'm going swimming," said Mrs. Haley. "Goodness, I hope I still can swim; I haven't tried since way back there when Jeff was little."

34

"Have you forgotten your surprise for Granny?" Mr. Haley asked.

"Oh, my goodness, yes! Pat, run in and get it."

"Thanks for reminding them, Bob. I was afraid I was going to mention it myself," Granny laughed.

"Do you promise to use this?" Pat asked, holding out a package.

"I do," Granny said as she took it. She opened the box and stared. "Is this my laying-out dress?" she joked.

"Granny, it's a swimsuit," Sam said reproachfully. "They also gave you a beach coat, see."

"I like this suit," said Granny firmly. "I like the beach robe too. I can even wear the robe in the water if I feel silly in the suit."

"Only the family will be in this cove," Jeff said.

"When I was a girl," reminisced Granny, "we wore stockings, underwear, bathing shoes . . . the whole bit."

"It's a wonder you didn't all drown," Jeff said.

"We didn't really swim. Oh, I did, because I was a country girl. All the others just splashed and screamed." Granny laughed at the remembrance.

Pat laughed with the rest, but she was

still thinking about the rock. Surely it must have been Kurt or Sam who had carried it out. But they had no time to chisel out that big rock. It *must* have been someone else.

"According to my schedule," said Mr. Haley, "Jeff and Pat will take their turn at cleaning up and doing the dishes. We'll need to do more fishing if we want enough to feed this gang."

Soon the camp was deserted except for Jeff and Pat. They cleared the table and swept the patio without much talking. But when Pat began washing dishes, she glanced out the window to be sure everyone was gone.

"I keep thinking how Mrs. Sweeny said those women saw the ghost of her husband carrying the rock. That was the last thing he did before he died."

"Was anyone else around when she told Dad that? Any neighbors?" Jeff threw back two forks he didn't think were clean enough.

"I'm not sure someone wasn't listening," Pat said slowly, washing the forks again.

"What do you mean?"

"I'd gone down to the dock and from there you can see an old boat shed or something. I was sure I saw a boy behind that shed. It seemed to me he was listening to Dad and Mrs. Sweeny talk."

Jeff threw down his towel. "I'll be right

back. Keep on washing," he said, and was out the door, heading for the steps that led down to the dock.

In a few minutes he was back. "I was afraid it might be too far to be heard," he explained, "but I don't believe it is. It's funny you can't see that shed from the patio. What did the guy look like?"

"Wait." Pat's forehead wrinkled in a deep frown. She stood, her hands still in the dishwater, then she grabbed Jeff.

"Now I remember! I thought at the time it might be the same boy we saw come out of the bushes when we were talking to Mr. Abbett."

"Mr. Abbett?"

"Yes, he's the man who lives in the big house way back in the woods from Mrs. Sweeny's. While we were talking to him, a boy jumped out of the bushes, started to say something to Mr. Abbett, and then jumped back in. He wore a tan cap pulled down over his ears and on his forehead."

"A boy? How old did he look?"

"All I remember about the kid was that tan cap pulled down low on a summer day. And that he looked mad—maybe because we'd seen him."

"But why should this guy try to play ghost for us?" Jeff threw back a tablespoon.

37

"If you keep throwing things back, we'll never get done," Pat snapped.

"Get them clean the first time. What if someone got a fork with egg on it? They'd know we did the dishes last. Now I wonder if maybe the Abbetts have kids?"

"I'll try to find out," Pat said, scrubbing hard at the tablespoon.

"We've got another thing that's sort of funny."

"What?"

"Mrs. Sweeny bringing down a gun. I never heard of a resort owner furnishing a gun before. Makes a person kind of uneasy."

"And how many resort owners have you heard of?" Pat demanded.

"About as many as you. I think we should get Kurt and Sam in on this."

"But if they're in on it, I'm out. You know that, Jeff. Kurt thinks girls are good for nothing and that their brains are the size of a small pea."

"Kurt might think that, but Sam doesn't and neither do I. So, what do you say?"

"I suppose we should tell them," sighed Pat. "But let's not go further than that. Maybe Dad, Mother, and Granny would want to leave. I don't want to spoil this vacation. Besides, when have we had a chance to solve a mystery?"

"I'll go along with that," Jeff agreed.

CHAPTER 4

Donnie surprised everyone that afternoon by getting up on the skis and staying there. He even made a graceful curve around the cove. Pat was still a little awkward and hated herself for falling twice. She *knew* she could have stayed up if she hadn't been trying so hard to show the boys how good she could be.

Later she sat on the dock and watched the boys perform. She didn't really want to watch them showing off, but she saw Mrs. Sweeny coming down to the dock to fish, and she'd learned to like the sad lady and her soft way of talking.

"They sure do like an audience," she said, waving her hand at the boys.

Mrs. Sweeny put down her can of bait and threw out her line. "They are very good. That slalom ski is hard to do." She looked absently at the boys. "Danny could use it when he was only six. He—" She stopped suddenly and glanced at Pat, who hadn't missed a word.

"Danny? Was he your son?"

Mrs. Sweeny tossed out her line again, reeling it slowly in. "Yes"

Her head was turned so that Pat could not see her face. Pat knew that she should take the hint and not stay on the same subject, but she didn't want to give up yet.

"Is he living with you now?"

"No, he's with his aunt, who lives about twenty miles from here." Mrs. Sweeny's voice was so soft Pat had to lean forward to hear her. Then she sighed deeply. "It was too—too sad for him after—I thought—his cousins would—" Her voice drifted off.

"I suppose he's happy there?" After the words were said Pat was ashamed. What had made her say anything that cruel?

She was surprised when she heard Mrs. Sweeny reply, "He's the age of the boys out there."

Pat looked out on the lake. Sam was skiing, and Kurt was astride his shoulders. The boys were laughing and yelling and so was their father, who was driving the boat.

"Just the same age," Mrs. Sweeny said again.

"I'll bet he loves to ski and swim," Pat said in a voice she hoped was encouraging.

Just then the bobber went down, and Mrs. Sweeny became busy pulling in a nice-sized crappie.

Granny and Mrs. Haley came down the

steps then. Granny was carrying a sack of string beans, Mrs. Haley had a big cooking pot.

"We thought it would be more fun to snap the beans here on the dock," Mrs. Haley said. "Mrs. Sweeny, why don't you eat with us this evening? We'd love to have you."

Mrs. Sweeny took her fish off the hook and smiled dimly. Her smiles never reached her eyes, Pat thought.

"Thank you, but I couldn't." She picked up her things and went up the steps. She stopped at the top to turn and say, "Thank you for asking me."

Just as they were ready to eat supper a rain storm blew up, so they filled their plates and looked for shelter. They ended up with the grown-ups and Donnie eating at the big cottage and Pat and the boys eating in the boys' cottage. It was while they were eating that Jeff told the story of the rock that had been moved.

Kurt and Sam listened, almost forgetting to eat. They were curious enough to get a flashlight and examine the rock.

"Neat job of chiseling." Sam said, as they hurried back in out of the rain.

"So the ghost that scared away the lady renters now wants to scare us off too," Kurt mused.

Sam frowned. "You know, if that wasn't such a big rock, I'd think maybe Mrs. Sweeny did it herself. She looks and acts weird."

"Isn't that a little silly? Why should she try to frighten away her renters?" Pat's voice was impatient, and Sam looked at her in surprise. He was used to Pat's agreeing with him.

"We never figured out why she brought the gun down either," Jeff said gloomily.

"Mrs. Sweeny is really very sweet," said Pat. "She has a boy—no—wait, Jeff, he isn't living with her. He's with an aunt."

"Did she tell you that?"

"Yes. She said something about it being too sad for him to be with her alone after his father died."

"Boy, she is something," said Kurt. "Wonder how the kid feels about that. How old is he, did she say?"

"About your age, she said."

"Where does the aunt live?" Jeff asked.

"I don't know. I was ashamed to ask too many questions."

"Gosh, this is fun!" Kurt gave a bounce on the cot. "Here we have a first-rate mystery right under our noses."

"Why doesn't she leave here?" he continued. "The people across the road wanted to buy this place, Dad said."

"There!" Jeff jumped up. "You have a reason *they* might want to scare us. If everyone gets scared off, Mrs. Sweeny will have to sell, right?"

"Do the Abbetts have any kids?" asked Sam.

Pat told him the story of the boy she had seen.

"I just hope whoever it is keeps on haunting," grinned Sam. "Won't he be surprised if we stay and stay?"

"I want to do more than stay. I want to catch him and tell him what I think of his haunting game." Kurt's voice was hard.

"Let's take turns watching," Sam suggested. "That way we'll soon know who it is."

"All night?" asked Pat. "Remember, we don't know what time he came last night."

"Don't you know what time Poochie barked and you went outside?" Sam asked.

"No," answered Jeff. "I didn't turn on the light to see, because I was afraid I'd wake Mom and Dad."

"Good thinking," said Kurt. "We don't want them to know anything about this. It might spoil their fun. And besides, it will be great trying to solve it ourselves."

"We could take turns," Pat said slowly. "I got the best place to watch, because the light is near my window, and I have a pretty good view of the wall." She didn't care too much about the job, but if she didn't offer to watch, she was sure the boys would go on with the whole thing without her.

"Good," said Sam. "You take your turn from bedtime until 2. I'll set my alarm for 1:30 and watch from then on until it gets light."

"No way," Kurt said flatly. "That wild alarm clock of yours would scare away a whole flock of ghosts."

"I'll put it under my pillow so no one will hear it but me."

"Another thing," asked Pat, "what do I do when whoever it is comes out?"

"She's right," Sam agreed. "What do I do if it appears on my watch?"

"I think the first time we just watch and see what he or she looks like. I can't imagine anyone being kooky enough to wear a sheet," Jeff said.

"The next night Jeff and I will watch," said Kurt. "By that time maybe we can figure out what we can do."

"I guess I'd better get back and shower and act like I'm sleepy," Pat said, getting up and putting the raincoat around her shoulders. She didn't have to pretend very long. The swimming that afternoon must have tired Granny because at 9:30 she was in bed sound asleep, her gentle snoring keeping time with the drip, drip of the rain off the eaves of the roof.

It was chilly sitting up, and Pat put a

sweater on over her pajamas. Poochie was not by the post on account of the rain. Donnie and Jeff had put a rug by their cots for him. The yard light glistened on the wet flagstones and the dog chain hanging on the steel post.

Pat pulled her little luminous clock nearer. She couldn't be getting sleepy — not yet. She'd better say her prayers now because she would be awfully sleepy by 2 o'clock. She even added a prayer for Mrs. Sweeny, but left it to God as to what Mrs. Sweeny might need most.

She had to admit that if someone could pick the right weather to haunt, this would certainly be the night. The wind moaned through the oaks on the vacant lot, and she could hear the slap of water on the boats.

Over in the big cottage a light was on, and Pat knew that her father was still reading. No use watching the bushes yet. No one would dare come out as long as that light was on. She glanced at the clock. It was only 10:30. How time dragged! She recited all the poetry she knew, but that only took 10 minutes.

The light in the big cottage finally went out, and Pat began to feel that odd tightening in the stomach muscles that she always got when she knew something exciting was going to happen. This might really be her chance to show the boys she was as smart as they were.

She strained her eyes toward those dark

bushes just beyond the rock wall. But soon they all seemed to run together, and she had to turn her eyes on the cottage to rest them. She was determined not to look at the clock.

Then she thought she saw something move near the wall. Yes! The bushes were moving – but that could be caused by the wind. The bushes kept moving and no one came out. It must be the wind, she decided.

If the Abbetts had some kids who liked to play pranks, she thought, moving a big rock might be their idea of fun. But then anger swept over her. This was beyond a cute prank. It could scare someone badly. Maybe Mrs. Sweeny had seen it once, and that was why she had brought down the gun.

Then, suddenly, several things began to happen at once, and Pat never could remember in what order. She heard the dog give a warning woof from off inside the house. Poochie didn't have to *see* anyone to know they were around. Then there was a tinkling sound like breaking glass, and the yard light went out.

Pat got up and felt her way to the door. It took her a while to get to the door in the dark and she opened it softly, not ever thinking what she would do when she got outside.

Then a small point of light came from the boys' cottage. Kurt or Sam must have heard that breaking glass too. The small flashlight skimmed over the patio. There was no one there, but there was a *big* round rock near the table. It took a second for it to sink into her mind. While she had slowly moved across two rooms, someone had grabbed the rock, put it down, and dashed away again.

Pat, watching the light, crossed to where the two boys were playing it over the bushes and weeds. Unfortunately it was too small and weak to do much good.

"Did you see it?" asked Sam.

"No. He must have carried that rock while the light was out," she whispered.

"We found out two things," Kurt said.

"He's fast and he's strong?" Sam guessed.

"Hold that light." Kurt pushed the light at Sam and took the rock to its place in the wall. Then, smooth and fast, he picked it up, ran with it to an open space on the patio, and dashed back to the wall again.

"Would you say I did that in the time it took you to find your way to the door in the darkness?" he asked Pat.

"It's hard to tell. It did take me a while, because I was afraid I'd stumble into something and wake Granny."

"Pat, where are you? What happened to the light?" As Granny's voice called, Pat ran as fast, or faster, than Kurt had.

47

"I guess it just went out," she said, as she went into the cabin. "It's awfully dark, isn't it?"

"You aren't in bed; I can tell."

"I wanted to be sure it wasn't raining in at the door."

"Well, good night again." Granny yawned, and Pat crawled into bed and began going over things that had happened that night.

CHAPTER 5

Pat awoke to the sound of cheerful voices. She sat up and looked out the window. Everyone was eating. Over on the wall the big rock was nicely in place. She might have thought the experience of the night before was a bad dream, except for the shattered glass of the light bulb near the pole.

She realized she was very hungry, jumped up, and threw on some clothes.

"How could anyone sleep with all this chattering?" Mrs. Haley made room for Pat to sit beside her.

They didn't see Mrs. Sweeny until she cleared her throat. She carried a light bulb box.

"I saw your light was out and brought you a new one. Would one of the boys climb up and replace it? I have a long stepladder at the house."

Pat wondered if Mrs. Sweeny had been watching for ghosts through the night too. She looked awfully tired. Why did she wear all that rouge? Someone ought to tell her it made her look older. But poor Mrs. Sweeny had no one to tell her.

Pat held out a hot buttered muffin, "Would you like this, Mrs. Sweeny? My mother is great at muffins."

For the first time Pat felt that Mrs. Sweeny was not looking by her, as she usually did, but was gazing at her directly.

"Thank you, dear. It looks delicious." She took the muffin, but did not eat it.

"The boys will be glad to replace the bulb," said Mr. Haley.

He walked over to the post. "It's shattered! We must have had a lot of wind last night."

Pat sucked in her breath and buttered another muffin.

"If I didn't know better, I'd have accused our boys of throwing rocks at it." Mr. Haley laughed, glancing at the boys who were busily eating.

"Not our idea of kicks, Dad," Jeff said, glancing at the others.

Mr. Haley turned to talk to Mrs. Sweeny, but she was gone. He shrugged and came back to the table. "Now she's here, now she's gone," he muttered as he sat down to his scrambled eggs.

"It must have been the wind," Mrs. Haley decided.

"Come to think of it, Pat and I noticed

the light was out last night," said Granny. "What time was that, Pat?"

"I'm sure I don't know." Pat took another big bite. She *didn't* know exactly, but even a half-lie bothered her a little.

"As soon as we've digested this wonderful breakfast," said Mr. Haley, "We'll get the snorkle and go out to the banks on the main arm of the lake. Don't forget the fins. We'll take turns doing scuba diving. But for right now, let's walk along the beach and find some pretty driftwood for Granny and Mother."

"I'll go with you," Donnie said quickly.

"Sorry about that, kid, but you and I are scheduled to clean camp," Kurt said.

"I'll take his place." Granny couldn't bear to see Donnie unhappy.

"No. It's sweet of you, Granny, but Donnie takes his turn just like the rest of us," Mr. Haley said firmly.

"We're going to take the station wagon and drive to town to do the laundry," said Mrs. Haley. "We also need groceries. If we aren't back by noon, there's plenty to make yourselves sandwiches. Granny and I might just eat lunch in town."

Donnie looked sadly at the table loaded with dirty dishes. "Why do we have to have such big breakfasts?"

"I saw you eat, so don't complain. Just

scrape and stack the plates. I'll fix the light."
Kurt tucked the light bulb in his T-shirt and
shinnied up the pole.

"She said she had a ladder," Donnie reminded his brother.

"We never use a ladder at home to put a
new bulb in our yard light."

"Boy, you sure can shinny."

"It's pretty from up here," Kurt said,
looking around after he'd put in the new bulb.
Then his eyes were caught by someone walking
up the path on the lot next to the cottages. This
person did not limp, nor was he middle-aged like
Mr. Abbett. He looked a little taller than Jeff
and wore an old straw hat.

Funny they'd never seen him before. He
could be an Abbett kid. Kurt was just about to
slide down the pole when he saw the boy look
up at him, then turn and run, disappearing into
the brush.

In a second Kurt had reached the ground
and was dashing across the patio.

"Where are you going?" Donnie cried,
following his brother. But Kurt was already
plunging into the heavy brush. He was angry.
Anyone running away like that was guilty of
something, and Kurt was determined to find
out what it was. When he got to the narrow
path, though, there was no one in sight. He
started up the hill toward the old shed Pat had

told him about. Then he slowed down. Actually, he had no business on Abbett's side of the cove.

"I can't get through," Donnie wailed trying to untangle himself from the heavy vines.

"Shut up! Who asked you to follow me?" Kurt loosened his brother impatiently. "Come on. Let's get back and clean up the dishes."

"But why did you run like that? Did you see something like a ghost?"

"Of course not. I thought I saw a boy, but maybe I didn't."

"I guess it was the same guy I saw yesterday," Donnie said, looking at a scratch on his arm.

Kurt had picked up a stack of plates, but he put them down again.

"Who did you see yesterday?"

"A guy about your age, I guess. I was fishing off the dock, and Poochie started barking, and I looked over there and saw this guy on the path. He sure looked mad. He was shooting at a tin can with a slingshot. Boy, was he good! He—"

"A slingshot!" Kurt looked at the yard light. "Of course. That would be easy if you could shoot at all."

"Are you talking to me?"

"No. Come on, let's get going. Then I'll help you with your diving. I watched you yesterday and you didn't look too good." Kurt went

into the big cottage with his stack of plates.

Donnie picked up a cup and saucer and followed his brother inside.

"Tell me, Donnie," said Kurt, "did that guy with the slingshot look very strong?"

"I didn't look at the muscles in his arm, but he sure could hit that tin can." Donnie held up a make-believe slingshot and aimed it out of the window. "Pang! pang!" he shouted.

"Will you *please* go out and bring in the rest of those things on the table. Try to carry more than one thing at a time, or we'll be in the kitchen all day."

Kurt began on the dishes. Outside he heard Donnie calling his dog and knew that if they were going to finish their work before noon, he would have to go out and get the rest of the dishes himself. He wondered if the boy he'd seen belonged to the people across the road. He'd have to think up an excuse to go over there soon.

Donnie was talking to someone, and Kurt dried his hands and went to the front of the cottage. Mrs. Sweeny stood there, holding a long stepladder. She gave Kurt a dim smile.

"I see you fixed the light without a ladder."

"No big deal, Mrs. Sweeny. Jeff and I always replace bulbs in our yard light. I'm sorry you had to drag that heavy thing down here. I'll take it back for you."

"No, I'll take it." She turned and started up the path, the end of the ladder scraping behind her.

"She sure must be strong for an old lady," Donnie said admiringly.

She *had* to be strong, Kurt agreed with Donnie.

"Mrs. Sweeny says that Poochie goes up to visit those people across the road," said Donnie. "I guess I'd better go get him. Wonder if they give him something to eat that makes him like it better there."

"Donnie, if you'd get in and help me, we'd get done before evening. Let's get our work done, and we'll both go to the neighbors to look for your dog."

CHAPTER 6

"Pat, will you go with me, please?"

Pat was reading, but suddenly she realized that Donnie had said that same thing about ten times.

"Where?"

"To that place on the hill across from where Mrs. Sweeny lives. My dog visits up there all the time, and I want to know why."

"Oh, Donnie, that's silly. He goes up there because he wants to. How can we find out what's in a dog's mind?" She reopened the magazine Granny had brought her from town.

"It's what's in those people's mind that I want to know. What are they giving my dog that makes him stay up there all the time?" Donnie turned to go up the rock steps. "Anyway, Kurt was very nice to me. He was *glad* to go up there with me, only he had no time. I'll bet he goes with me later on."

Pat looked up curiously. "You say Kurt *wanted* to go with you to see the Abbetts?"

"He said so."

"Come on, I'll go with you." Pat closed her magazine and followed Donnie up the steps.

This might be her chance to find out about the Abbetts. If Kurt was "glad" to go, it was probably for the same reason.

"Mrs. Sweeny must be scared someone's going to get in her house," Donnie remarked as they went past the tightly closed building.

"It does seem sort of funny."

Donnie always hated to leave anything with a question mark. Even if he didn't know an answer, he made one up.

"Maybe her dead husband gave her some diamonds to keep," he decided.

"Dead people give nothing. You know that." Pat glanced at the mailbox and read the name of Hank R. Sweeny.

"Before he was dead he gave them to her and he said, 'Always keep everything locked up tight and—'"

"Come on," Pat said, taking Donnie's hand and crossing the road. They walked up the long driveway that led to the neighbor's house. It looked as if the grass had never been cut so it turned to weeds instead. The large rambling house loomed gloomy and deserted far back in the shade of the big oaks.

"I don't think we should have come alone," Pat said, looking at the big house.

"Why not? Do you see Poochie?"

"No, I don't. We're going no farther. We

know nothing about these people. You yell for Poochie. He'll hear you if he's around."

Donnie opened his mouth wide and yelled. The dog didn't come, but someone opened the front door and came onto the porch. Pat recognized him as the man her father had talked to when they rented the cottages. Pat didn't know whether to turn and run or not, but the closer the man came the more she could see he didn't look fierce or mean.

"My brother is looking for his dog," Pat explained. "Have you seen him?"

"Yeah, he was here this morning. He's a nice dog. Must be in the woods now."

"We don't want him to bother you, or your family." Pat figured that ought to get some information.

"No family here. Just me and Paul. He's my nephew, but he's gone all day and mostly all evenings. He works at the marina in town. Makes good money for such a young man. At home here, all he does is eat and sleep. That's why I get kind of lonesome, and your dog coming to see me is nice. I sometimes give him bits of my food."

"Oh, but Poochie only eats dog food. He's not supposed to eat table snacks," Donnie worried.

Pat squeezed Donnie's arm and smiled at Mr. Abbett. "I'm sure you don't give him too much food. We're glad if he keeps you company sometimes, aren't we, Donnie?" She pinched Donnie harder.

"Sure! Sure — only don't give him potatoes or beans," Donnie warned in spite of the pinches.

"I'll watch that. But I can't see as a few bites from my plate is going to hurt him. We had a dog just ate leavings, and he got to be 15 years old before he died, so I reckon —"

Just then there was a crackling of dead leaves in the brush and Poochie bounded out. He ran first to Mr. Abbett and licked his hand before he came to Donnie.

Donnie was hurt and showed it. Pat said quickly, "We'd better go. Nice seeing you again Mr. Abbett. Maybe someday we can meet your son."

"Nephew, His daddy and mom drowned in the lake in a storm. They'd bought a cheap little boat that got swamped in the waves. Storms git bad hereabouts. Anyways, I took him and he lived here, helping me, but now he's old enough to earn money of his own."

Pat wondered how old that was and if the boy really only ate and slept at Mr. Abbett's.

"It was nice of you to take care of him," Donnie made himself say, although he was still hurt.

"I think maybe we've seen your nephew on the path to the lake several times," ventured

Pat. She didn't miss the strange look that came over Mr. Abbett's face. Uneasily his eyes swept the woods beside them.

"Let's go home, Poochie," Donnie said, taking a firm hold on the dog's collar. "Goodbye," he remembered to say as he started toward the road.

"Seen any haunts yet?" Mr. Abbett called after him.

"No, we haven't seen any ghosts," Pat answered.

Donnie stopped and turned. "My dog would bark at a ghost if he saw one, because he hasn't ever seen one. I haven't—"

"Come on, Donnie." Pat took her brother's hand and pulled him toward the road. She was thinking about that nephew. Mr. Abbett had said he worked all day and most evenings. But why had he looked so funny when Pat said she thought they'd seen the nephew on the path? Was he lying? If he wasn't, then who had they seen?

"He could have sneaked out at night while his uncle was asleep." She didn't know she'd thought out loud until Donnie looked up at her.

"Who sneaked?"

"Nothing. What are you going to do about your dog? You can't tie him up all day and all night too."

"I guess not. I hope it won't hurt Poochie to get a few scraps from Mr. Abbett. It's nice of my dog to cheer him up."

That evening the boys and Pat got together again in the boys' cottage. It wasn't raining, but it was too cool to sit outside and everyone was too tired to carry wood for a big fire.

Kurt told his story of seeing the boy, and Pat told of their visit to Mr. Abbett.

"If his uncle wants to buy this place, the kid might have the idea that if he haunts whenever Mrs. Sweeny gets renters, soon she'll have to sell," Jeff suggested.

"Mr. Abbett looked awfully funny when I said we saw his nephew," said Pat.

"I'm staying with Mrs. Sweeny as a suspect," Sam maintained.

"That rock's heavy, and Mrs. Sweeny is small," argued Pat. "Besides, why on earth would she rent this place and then try to get rid of people?"

"She's weird, I tell you," said Sam. "Did you ever look her directly in the eye? She's there somewhere, but it never gets as far as her eyes."

"She's strong enough to carry a rock. You should have seen her carry that heavy ladder," Kurt put in.

"When are we going to tell Dad?" Pat asked.

"We don't know much yet," replied Kurt. "This is fun, unraveling a mystery."

"As long as the ghost doesn't do more than tote a rock back and forth, let's keep it a secret," Sam agreed.

"He probably won't do that any more. Not if he stayed to watch you running back with it last night," Pat said.

"Maybe not, Anyway, tonight I'm going to watch." Sam pulled his chair closer to the group and spoke softly, as he too thought someone could be listening.

"Pat and Jeff, when you go back to your cottages, I'll slip out with you and hide in the shadows. Then Kurt can close up the place as usual. You'll have to talk to yourself, Kurt, so that they think I'm still inside. Right?"

"And how!" Kurt's eyes sparkled. "Where are you going to hide?"

"In the bushes right behind the wall where the loose rock is. Poochie will be tied up at the usual place, but he won't bark at me. I'll certainly be close enough to that rock to know when it's picked up."

"Do you want me, too?" Jeff asked hopefully.

"It's a job for only one person, not a bunch of people. Besides, you'd be sure to wake Mom or Dad, getting out of that cottage, and then we'd have to spill the whole story." Kurt was talking

63

in that big brother voice that Jeff thoroughly disliked.

"He got out without waking them the other night," Pat reminded him. "Besides, did it ever cross your mind that whoever it is might not like Sam's playing Peeping Tom with him? Suppose he jumps on him?"

"I'll be ready for him." Sam said it so gleefully that Kurt and Jeff envied him.

"I'll be there in a second if you get in trouble," Kurt promised.

"I'm going to bed and sleep," Pat said. "But don't you do anything dangerous, Sam." She ran across the patio and listened before she opened the door. But Granny was sitting under the lamp reading her prayer book. She didn't talk until after Pat had showered and brushed her hair. Then Granny put the prayer book on top of her Bible.

"Why are you smiling, Granny?" asked Pat.

"Because I almost prayed for my chickens tonight. Now isn't *that* something to bother God with?"

"I guess it would be. I do prayers like that too. I don't think God minds."

Granny watched Pat brush her hair. "Pat, would you do something for me?"

"Of course. What is it?"

"Sing Sam's evening prayer for me."

64

"Let's sing it together."

After the lights were out they softly sang the little evening song, and Pat wondered if, in his mind, Sam was singing with them.

Much later, after she had been asleep, Poochie's barking right below her window awakened her. She sat bolt upright and saw the dog straining at his chain and barking furiously at the stone wall. Someone was there. He wouldn't bark at Sam. Pat grabbed the blanket off her bed and wrapped it around her. Noiselessly she went out the door and rushed across the patio.

Kurt and Sam were standing beside the wall. The rock was still in its place.

"I *had* him! I tell you, I had him, but he was wearing some sort of slicker, and it was so slippery he just slid out of my hands like a greased pig." Sam was breathless and angry.

"Shhh! You'll have the whole family up. Come on. We'll try another time." Kurt pushed his friend toward the cottage.

Pat gave Poochie a comforting pat and crept inside. This ghost business was keeping her from getting her sleep. How she wished that Sam had held onto him—or her.

CHAPTER 7

Jeff too had heard Poochie barking, and he held his breath for fear the noise would wake his parents. But no one stirred, and Jeff finally got up and went to the window. Just then the cot on which Donnie slept gave a squeek, followed by a loud thump. Jeff knew exactly what had happened, and he went over to help a still sleeping Donnie back into bed.

"He knocked me off the dock," Donnie murmured.

"No, you fell out of your bed again. Go back to sleep before you wake Mom and Dad."

It seemed that Jeff had hardly gone back to sleep when he heard his parents stirring and remembered that they had decided to go fishing at daybreak. They talked in whispers and were very quiet, but Jeff was wide awake now and was glad they were leaving. He decided to run over to the boys' cottage as soon as his parents were safely away.

He went to the window and saw his father walking across the patio with his fishing tackle. Jeff watched as his dad's old fishing hat disappeared over the hill. Soon his mother followed, but then they collided because Mr. Haley was already returning.

"The fishing boat's gone!" Mr. Haley was too excited to lower his voice.

"The fishing boat?" Mrs. Haley asked in a dazed voice. "But what could have happened to it?"

Jeff pulled on shorts and ran outside. "What's wrong, Dad?"

"The fishing boat is gone," Mr. Haley repeated.

Jeff ran down the steps, not even noticing how cold the dew felt on his bare feet. Mr. Haley followed him down to the dock.

"I can't believe it. Its a fairly new boat and in good condition. There are no leaks at all. I had it out yesterday and the bottom was bone dry."

"Dad, look!" Jeff held up the rope to which the boat had been tied.

"Why it's been cut!" Mr. Haley muttered. "Look, Jeff, there's no doubt about it. Someone has stolen our boat. This rope's cut." He held the rope in his hand and showed it to his wife as she came down the steps.

Jeff ran past his mother, up to the boys' cottage. "Hey, get up! Someone's stolen the fishing boat!" he yelled.

The boys bounded out immediately. They'd already dressed and headed straight for the lake. By this time it was full daylight. Pat and Granny were awake too and joined the group on the dock. Only Donnie slept through it all.

"Who would steal a boat?" Mr. Haley asked, shaking his head in disbelief. "It's dangerous! These boats are all registered, I'm sure."

"Let's go up and get breakfast," suggested his wife. "By that time Mrs. Sweeny should be up and maybe she can shed some light on the mystery." She and Granny went back up the steps.

"I just don't get it." Mr. Haley stared at the cut rope. Sam and Kurt looked at each other, and when Sam nodded, Kurt turned to his father.

"Dad, I guess it's time we tell you about a few things happening around here. But let us go and grab a few more clothes first. It's cold."

Mr. Haley nodded, his eyes still on the rope.

Later, when they were dressed and waiting for breakfast, Kurt told him of the supposed ghost who moved rocks and how Sam had almost had him the night before.

Pat added her information and so did Jeff. Mrs. Haley and Granny looked worried, and Mr. Haley's voice was grave.

"I'm glad you finally told me. Sam, didn't you realize you might have been hurt?"

"No sir, since the boy they saw was no bigger than we were."

"But you don't know if it was the boy you've been seeing. The person who is evidently trying to scare us away might be someone else."

Sam nodded. "You're right. I thought for a while it could be Mrs. Sweeny, except when she brought that shotgun down, she certainly must have realized that someone here might use it on a prowler and that the rock carrier would have been in danger of being shot."

"Whoever is involved," mused Mr. Haley, "is the sort of person who steals boats. That's certainly more serious than carrying rocks. I think it's time Mrs. Sweeny and I had a long talk."

"If someone like that is around, I'd hate to leave any of the children here alone," said Mrs. Haley.

"Now, honey, aren't you being a little hasty? We'll soon get the whole thing in the open. I'll have a talk right now with Mrs. Sweeny."

Mrs. Haley walked to the top of the hill where she could look down on the dock where Donnie was tossing sticks into the water for Poochie to retrieve.

"Let's keep this — this story from Donnie,"

she suggested. "You know how he worries about anything we can't explain."

"I don't like things like that either because they make me *mad.* Anyone who tries to scare people just for the heck of it is plain mean, and I wish I'd been with Sam when he grabbed whoever it was. I'd—" Pat faltered, not knowing exactly what she would have done.

"This is no job for a girl," Kurt said.

"Why, Kurt Haley, you—"

"Never mind, both of you," said Mr. Haley. "It's not a job for either of you. After the boat trick I think this is a job for the police. But I don't want to go to them before I talk to Mrs. Sweeny."

"We won't let it bother us," Granny said calmly. "As soon as Bob comes back from seeing Mrs. Sweeny, you and he go fishing like you planned, Ruth. As for me, as soon as the kitchen is cleaned up, I'm going to do some baking. I get these crazy urges once in a while."

"I'm glad you get them," Donnie said as he came to the top of the steps. "I hope your urge has chocolate in it?"

"It has," Granny laughed, ruffling Donnie's hair.

Pat got her magazine and went down on the dock to read and soak up sun. When school started in the fall, she knew the girls would

71

compare suntans, and she was determined to be the brownest of all.

Mr. Haley had gone up the hill toward Mrs. Sweeny's house, and Pat could hear Granny and her mother talking about how they were going to chill a huge watermelon they had bought in town.

"I hate cutting it all up," her mother was saying. "Besides, we just about filled up all the spaces in the refrigerator with the meat and fresh vegetables and fruit."

"I've got an idea," Kurt said. "Listen to this, Sam. Have you noticed how the water gets cooler when you dive down?"

Sam nodded.

"Well, going on that, I'd think the further you go down the colder it would be."

Sam shrugged, waiting for one more of Kurt's brilliant ideas.

"So, why not lower the watermelon down in the water, out from the cove where the water is deep. We leave it there for several hours; then we pull it up, and we have a fine chilled watermelon."

"It sounds good," Sam agreed. "But how will you lower it?"

"With a stone in a gunnysack, with a rope tied to it and a bobber on the top to show us where it is. I read once that that's the way they mark the lobster beds in Maine."

"It won't hurt to try," Mrs. Haley said a little doubtfully.

Some minutes later Sam and Kurt came down with a gunnysack. Inside was the huge watermelon and the stone.

"Chilled watermelon for supper tonight," Kurt said happily. They put the sack in the boat and soon were out to the opening of the cove. Pat watched as they lowered it into the water.

"I've a feeling we'll never see that watermelon again," Mrs. Haley said, watching from the dock.

"Why?" Donnie asked.

"I don't know, I just have that feeling. Well, who cares? What's one 99-cent watermelon? It's probably no good anyway. I never could pick out a ripe watermelon."

"What's going on here?" Mr. Haley asked, coming down the steps.

"The boys put a watermelon in deep water to chill it," replied his wife. "We had no room in the refrigerator."

"Well, we might as well go fishing. Mrs. Sweeny is either sound asleep or gone, and I have no intention of sitting around all day waiting for her. Get ready, Ruth, and as soon as the boys get back, we'll go."

Mrs. Haley ran up the steps. The boys gunned the boat's motor and came back to the dock.

"How are you going to find that melon?" Mr. Haley asked.

"See that little red bobber?" replied Kurt. "All we have to do is drive out and pull the melon up. Isn't that a clever idea?"

"No," said his father shortly. "You've put it too far out. Someone will ski over it and cut the rope."

"He's right," Sam said. "Let's go out and get it and sink it near the dock. Gosh, this water's deep enough."

So they went out again, pulled up the melon and repeated the routine, sinking the melon 4 or 5 feet from the dock. Then Mr. and Mrs. Haley climbed into the boat with their gear and soon were out of sight around the bend.

Pat thought about the boat and about poor Mrs. Sweeny. Her blood boiled when she thought of someone's hating Mrs. Sweeny so much that they'd steal a good boat. What would such a person try next? How she'd love to find out who it was all by herself. Restlessly she closed her magazine and climbed the steps. Poochie and Donnie were playing their version of hide-and-seek. Jeff and Sam were playing catch. Wonderful smells poured from the kitchen in the larger cottage and Pat went in to see Granny. There sat two pies, ready to pop into the oven as soon as the brownies had baked.

"What are you doing inside on a day like

74

this?" Granny demanded. "You tired of swimming?"

"No, but it's not much fun alone," sighed Pat. "Kurt went with Dad and Mom, and the other kids are busy. Do you think you'd have enough brownies to fill a small plate? I'd like to take a few to Mrs. Sweeny."

Granny nodded her approval. "I think that's a real nice idea. I'll fix her a plate as soon as they cool."

"She looks so sad, Granny."

"She is sad. But your father said she wasn't home, so why don't you wait a little while to take her the brownies?"

Pat went out on the cottage steps and watched the boys play catch. Sam invited her to join them, but she refused. Soon Granny came out with the plate of brownies covered with a paper napkin.

"Better not say anything to Mrs. Sweeny about the boat, Pat," she cautioned. "Your father will want to talk to her about that."

When Pat got to the top of the hill she saw that the house was still tightly closed and all the blinds flush with the sills. But she went to the front anyway and knocked on the screen. She knew Mrs. Sweeny had to be inside because the door was locked from the inside. After a long wait, she had just about decided to go back to the cottages when she heard the click of the door latch and Mrs. Sweeny stood on the other side of the screen door.

"I brought you some brownies Granny baked today. They're awfully good."

Mrs. Sweeny's face lost some of its tight look. She even managed a smile as she looked at Pat.

"They smell delicious." Mrs. Sweeny seemed to hesitate, then she unlocked the door and stepped back. "Come in, dear. I'm not used to having company."

Pat stepped inside, and a wave of hot stale air closed around her. To her dismay Mrs. Sweeny closed and locked both doors behind her. It made Pat feel uneasy.

Her face must have betrayed her, because Mrs. Sweeny said, "You never know what sort of—" Suddenly she stopped. "Oh, why am I lying to you?" she asked in a shaky voice.

Pat jumped. "Lying?" she said uncertainly.

Mrs. Sweeny had been crying, she noticed. There were little runways of tears over the rouge. Pat wished she hadn't come. She hated to see people sad.

"You might as well see now that you're here," Mrs. Sweeny said, waving to a room on the left of the hall.

Pat never forgot the first glance into the front room. It was just the ordinary run of front rooms, a divan, two matching chairs, a television set, and a beige rug. But all the upholstery was slashed so that the padding was spilling out on the floor. The draperies were hanging in long ragged strands. The rug had cuts in it, and the wooden floor showed through. The walls were covered with splashes of paint.

"It's terrible, isn't it?" asked Mrs. Sweeny weakly. "They've ruined everything I own. Come into the kitchen."

Pat was so shocked she followed Mrs. Sweeny like a mechanical doll. She put the plate of brownies on the table, and they promptly slid off and spilled on the floor. Then she saw why. One leg had been cut off much shorter than the other three. The flooring where the brownies scattered was cut up and broken off.

Mrs. Sweeny went to the refrigerator. Inside, it looked as though someone had taken an ice pick and punched holes all over.

"I have no way of keeping food cool anymore, so I just eat out of cans. The stove too has been ruined." Mrs. Sweeny spoke in a dull flat voice as though she were reading something out of the paper.

Pat gazed at the wallpaper, which hung in shreds, and the frayed and torn curtains. She could not get her vocal chords to work.

"Now you can see why I brought down a gun that first night you were here," said Mrs.

Sweeny. I was afraid they might start on the cottages next. I sit up all night going from window to window watching for them. But they've only come when I was gone, so I don't go anywhere now. I've everything locked up and I don't know how they get in."

Pat still could not speak, but Mrs. Sweeny didn't seem to notice. "It first began the week before you came to look at the place. They cut the wires to the phone."

"They? Who?" Pat finally managed to croak.

Mrs. Sweeny nodded toward the front of the house. "Who else? They wanted to buy it, and when I wouldn't sell, they started this so that I'd have to."

"Did you go to the police?"

"At first I waited, but when they kept on ruining things I went to the sheriff. He wouldn't do anything. I know he's a friend of theirs." Again she nodded in the direction of the Abbetts' house. "I had hope when I saw the sheriff go over there once, but I guess it was just a friendly visit because he didn't come here to see my place."

Pat shuddered. The ruined kitchen and the hot stale air made her a little sick. She felt tears drop off her chin. "Mrs. Sweeny, it's horrible. Let me tell my father. He'll want to help you, I know."

"No one can help me; I'm just glad Danny isn't here," Mrs. Sweeny said in her hopeless voice.

Pat wondered if she should tell about the boat, but she couldn't bring herself to bring any more grief to the miserable woman. Instead she stepped forward to put a comforting hand on Mrs. Sweeny's arm. Then she stepped on a brownie and backed up.

"Oh, your lovely cookies are ruined! Everything is ruined!" Mrs. Sweeny sobbed, not even trying to hide her face.

"I'm going to leave now," said Pat shakily. "But believe that we will help you."

Mrs. Sweeny didn't seem to hear her, so Pat went through the hall and unlocked both doors. She hesitated and called back. "You want to lock up after me?"

When no answer came, she went out. She heard both locks click as she started down the hill to the cottages.

CHAPTER 8

Mr. and Mrs. Haley were coming up the steps when Pat got back from her visit to Mrs. Sweeny.

"Fishing no good?" Sam called.

"Sun's too hot," replied Mr. Haley. "Besides, I didn't feel right about going off and not telling about that boat. I'll go right up and get it off my mind."

"Dad, wait!" said Pat. "I've something to tell you before you go."

"Why, Pat honey, you're shaking! What happened?" asked Granny.

Pat told her story to the entire family, even Donnie, whose eyes grew larger and larger.

"It's so terrible, horrible," she finished, shuddering. "Everything's ruined. How can people be so *mean?* And that Mr. Abbett acts so friendly."

"I'm not going to let my dog go up there anymore," Donnie declared.

"Now wait. We don't know for sure if Mr. Abbett and his nephew are doing this," Mr. Haley warned.

"But she *said* so," Pat cried.

"Did she say she saw them?"

"No, she didn't," Pat admitted.

Mr. Haley stood. "I'll go up right now." He shook his head. "I wish I were a Solomon; I don't know how to handle this."

"Want me to go with you?" Mrs. Haley offered.

"Not now. Maybe later I'll bring her down. Also, since she has no telephone, I'll take her to town — to the sheriff if I can."

"I don't want my dad to go alone," Donnie worried.

"He's going to see a poor old widow. Do you think she's going to shoot him?" Kurt asked in disgust.

Mrs. Haley watched her husband until he made the turn and was out of sight. "If I didn't feel we should stay and help this poor woman, I'd want to pack up and leave tomorrow."

"But, Mom, all this stuff is being done to Mrs. Sweeny, not to us," protested Jeff.

"But Pat said everything in her house was ruined. That's probably why they started on the boats. Heavens knows what's next."

"I'm going in and start lunch," Granny said firmly.

"Oh, goody! Those pies looked wonderful," said Donnie.

"The pies are too hot to eat for lunch,"

Granny replied. "I want them for supper. The boys can pull up the watermelon now."

Both boys looked down from the cove. "The bobber's gone," Kurt yelled. "Granny, was anyone skiing in our cove this morning?"

"Think I heard two or three boats."

"That's right," added Jeff. "We saw them while we were playing catch. Remember, Sam, the big show-off that buzzed our dock?"

"Come on, guys! We've got to do some deep sea diving. Bring the snorkel and fins." Kurt was happy. He loved anything exciting.

"He acts like he's going to pull up the Queen Elizabeth," Pat said in disgust, watching her brother dash down the steps.

Pat went into the cottage to help get lunch. It was funny how she loved to be near Granny and Mother when she was worried.

"I'll devil the eggs, Granny," she offered, and Granny handed her a big pot of hard-cooked eggs.

"Poor Mrs. Sweeny," sighed her mother. "It's horrible. I can't think of anything worse than not having my family around me and being hounded like she is."

"But Pat said she had a boy," Granny said.

"Yes, she said he was about the age of our big boys."

"He should be here with his mother.

That's the joy of a family. You share your joys and sorrows alike. It's part of growing up." Granny was peeling an onion for the potato salad, and tears ran down her face.

Then they heard shouts from the lake. Kurt's voice was the loudest and grew even louder as he reached the patio and ran across it to the house. He entered the kitchen, panting so hard he couldn't speak.

"You're dripping over everything, Kurt," his mother scolded, "Dry off before you bring the watermelon in."

"We didn't find the watermelon," Kurt gasped.

"You didn't?"

"We found the boat! The boat's been sunk, right there by the dock!" Kurt managed to get out.

"Can we get it up?" Pat asked.

"If we all help. Mom and Granny can pull from the dock and the rest of us can try to get it high enough and turn it over."

"You want me too?" Donnie asked eagerly from the door.

"Yes. Get on your trunks and come down." Kurt turned and ran.

"Something happening all the time," Granny smiled as she wiped up the big pool of water Kurt had dripped on the floor. "Come on, Ruth. Off we go."

Pat ran for her swimsuit, and soon they were all in the water except Granny and Mrs. Haley. It wasn't too bad pulling the boat up, but it took a lot of doing to turn the boat over. Once this was done, with everyone helping, they finally got the boat on the dock, upside down. There was a big slash in the bottom of it.

Just then Mr. Haley came running down the steps.

"Look, Dad, we found it!" cried Jeff. "Someone cut the rope and then slashed a hole, so the boat sank."

Mr. Haley examined the hole. "That's what it looks like. Well, I'd rather have that than have it stolen. No doubt, someone can repair this."

"Did you get to talk to Mrs. Sweeny?" asked Mrs. Haley.

"No, I've been up there all this time, waiting for her."

"But, Dad, she's got to be there! She says she goes nowhere," Pat said.

"Then she's sleeping with a pillow over her ears."

"I guess she must have to sleep during the day because she guards her house all night."

"So what are we going to do?" Sam asked.

"You're going to come up and eat lunch. We've got an especially good one," Mrs. Haley said, starting up the steps.

"But the watermelon?" Kurt asked.

"You're not going diving for it now. All of you are tired. How about eating warm pie, Granny? Then we can feed on chilled water-melon this evening."

"They should be cool enough by now," Granny agreed.

After lunch Mr. Haley went up to Mrs. Sweeny's house again. He was gone a long time, and when he finally came back, he looked unhappy.

"Can't talk her into going to the sheriff. She's convinced that it's the Abbetts and she can't do a thing. When I told her about the boat, she seemed almost to have expected it."

"She did?" Sam asked quickly. "You don't think she could be so mixed up that she does these things herself, maybe sleep-walking or something?"

"I'm not sure of anything. I feel so help-less. Something should be done, but I can't go to the sheriff if she tells me not to."

"We'll think it over for today. Maybe the answer will come to us tonight," Mrs. Haley said gently. "Don't you agree with me, Granny?"

"Yes."

They had a quiet afternoon. It had gotten much warmer and they all went swimming. Later, they skied, all but Pat. She was dis-couraged about her skiing, and she could not get her mind off of Mrs. Sweeny. The more she thought of someone trying to get rid of Mrs. Sweeny, the angrier she got.

That evening as she got ready for bed Granny asked, "Pat, are you afraid?"

"Afraid? Of what?" Pat stopped brushing her teeth.

"Of whoever is doing this to your friend, Mrs. Sweeny."

"No, I'm not afraid," Pat said earnestly, "I'm *mad,* just plain mad."

"Funny, but when something bothers me, something I can't figure out, I just pray before I go to sleep and ask God for the solution."

"And in the morning you know the answer?" Pat asked.

"Almost always. So why don't we do that for poor Mrs. Sweeny."

"All right, we'll both try it. But, Granny," Pat said, leaning to kiss the wrinkled cheek, "you sound like God's a sort of computer. He comes up with the answers."

"A computer with heart and love," Granny agreed. "Call Him what you want, child. He's there, and He knows the answers."

But in spite of her prayers Pat tossed and turned on her little narrow cot. She could still see the wrecked house, and it burned inside her like glowing coals. Someone *had* to get whoever did it. Didn't the boys worry? They hadn't said one word about watching for the so-called ghost that night. Then it was up to her, Pat. She'd watch and she'd *do* something.

After she was sure Granny was asleep, Pat sat on the side of her cot and stared at the bushes behind the wall, fiercely wishing she would see them move. What she would do if they did didn't seem to worry her. All she wanted was to do *something*. She sat up straighter, straining her eyes. The bushes only tossed lightly in the breeze from the lake, but it seemed she saw a lighter blur over near the steps.

Poochie, sleeping below the light, suddenly raised his ears, and a deep growl rumbled inside him. That did it! Without really thinking what she was going to do, Pat grabbed a blanket to wrap around her. Granny was sound asleep, as she tiptoed to the door and went out. She didn't cross the patio but stayed in the shadows of the yard light; and, brushing the walls of the cottage, she went to the back, crossing to the next cottage, where she had a good view of the top of the steps.

Yes, someone was moving on the steps. Whoever it was also stayed just on the fringe of light, not much more than a blur that soon disappeared down the steps.

Pat felt no fear. This mean person was going down to the boat dock. No doubt he wanted to sink another boat, or the same one again.

She flitted to the steps and reached them just as the figure got down to the dock. He wore swimming trunks and was stooping to the rope of the boat they used to ski. There was enough light so that Pat could watch him. He was cutting away at the rope; she could hear the sawing sound.

At first she crouched down on the steps so that if he turned he would not see her outlined against the light. Then she shrugged off the blanket, getting ready to run to the big cottage to get her father. But as she half rose, she glanced back. The figure had an axe and was swinging it high. There was no time to think. Pat flew down the steps, dragging the blanket with her. Although she made no sound, the figure must have sensed her coming, because he paused and turned. With a cry Pat leaped, hitting him with all of her one hundred pounds. He was knocked flat on his stomach and Pat sat astride him. She still had the blanket, which she promptly pulled over his head and face. Then she screamed.

Afterwards the boys said that scream could have been heard in Asia, but the important thing was that everyone in camp heard it — except Donnie.

Meanwhile Pat could not hold the figure down. He twisted and turned, knocking her back. By that time her father was yelling.

"Pat, where are you?"

"Dock!" Pat screamed, trying to grab the figure's legs as he scrambled to his feet. He gave her a hard shove and jumped in the water.

Mr. Haley was running down the steps, a big flashlight in his hand. The boys were right behind him and, seeing the swimmer, they both jumped in after him. Mr. Haley followed them with the light from the dock. They were gaining on the boy, although he was swimming with powerful strokes. He got to the broken dock and scrambled up, but the boys were right behind and grabbed him.

"Darling, are you hurt?" Mrs. Haley asked as Pat lifted her hand to her jaw.

"Not much. He did give me a wallop though."

"Look at that kid's hair," Mr. Haley said, still focusing the light on the three boys.

Pat turned to look. "Why it's red, blazing red, even at night."

Sam and Kurt were tearing through the brush, the boy between them. Mr. Haley went to meet them.

"Who are you?" he asked.

"It's none of your business." The boy's eyes were flashing, his voice sullen.

"I'm making it my business, young man. Your little games are over. Now you march up there with the boys, and we'll hear your story."

Pat and Jeff followed the others up the steps. Jeff looked at Pat admiringly. "You tackled him all by yourself."

Pat nodded. "Jeff, does he remind you of someone?"

But the boy was talking, "I don't have to tell you *anything*. I didn't hurt you or any of your stuff, and I'm not going to tell you one thing."

"Come to our cottage. Donnie's still asleep," Sam suggested.

They sat on the floor and on the sides of the cots. Mr. Haley stood facing the boy.

"If you won't talk to us, I'll be forced to call the sheriff."

"How?" He tipped his head toward the house on the hill. "She's not got a phone."

"Who are you?" Mr. Haley asked again.

"I'll tell you who he is," Sam said suddenly. "He's Mrs. Sweeny's son."

Looking at him more carefully, he did look like Mrs. Sweeny.

"Kurt, go up to the house and get Mrs. Sweeny," said Mr. Haley.

"No!" Like a steel spring the boy jumped, his eyes blazing. "Don't you dare call her down here. I don't want her here."

"Will you talk?"

The boy nodded sullenly, and Kurt gave

a sigh of relief. He had visions of Mrs. Sweeny aiming her shotgun out of the window if she saw him coming and didn't recognize him.

"Did you not only play ghost but damage your mother's furniture?" demanded Mr. Haley.

"Yes, but I can't see why it has anything to do with you."

"You ruined everything!" Pat gasped, holding her jaw. "How could you be so mean to your own mother?"

"Where does your aunt live?" Mrs. Haley asked gently.

"About 20 miles from here. My mother sent me there after—my dad died. You know why?" He looked directly at Mrs. Haley. "She said it wasn't good for me to be alone here with her, so out I went." Some of the hardness went out of his face. "You wouldn't do that to your kids, would you?"

"Weren't you happy at your aunt's?" Mrs. Haley asked.

The boy did not take his eyes from her face. "She had six kids and a little house. She didn't have too much money." His eyes flashed again. "Besides, *this* was my home. I was kicked out of my home by my mother. Some mother!" He looked sullenly at his bare feet, a shudder shaking him.

Mrs. Haley got up, took a blanket from

the cot, and wrapped it around his shoulders. His eyes softened again. "Thanks."

"Boys, you get on dry clothes, too, or wrap blankets around you."

Mr. Haley made no move to talk, but nodded to his wife. "How did you get here?" she asked softly. "Won't your aunt worry about you?"

"I told her I was going home. She was nice to me, but I think she was glad she had one less mouth to feed."

"Were you the one that frightened those women?" Mrs. Haley asked.

A flicker of a smile crossed his freckled face. "Yes. I'd just gotten here. How those silly women yelled! I figured if I scared everyone away, my mother'd have to sell; and we'd move away and be a family again, even if there was only the two of us."

"Where are you staying?"

"At the Abbetts. They've always been nice to me, so I'm staying with them."

"Do you know your mother is blaming Mr. Abbett and his nephew for all the awful things you did to her furniture?" Pat asked.

His anger flared again. "Why should she think that? All he wanted to do was to buy the place. She can't keep it up by herself. And I won't ever stay here. This place killed my dad, and I want to move to the city. But she won't listen. *She won't listen!*" he almost shouted. "She'd rather live with a dead husband than a live son."

"What is your name?" Mr. Haley asked.

"Dan Sweeny." He said it proudly, straightening his broad shoulders under the blanket. "Anyway, then you came and you wouldn't get scared. One of you big guys almost had me one night." He looked from Kurt to Sam.

"It took a girl to get you," Kurt said.

The boy jerked, but did not answer. He looked at Pat, and she quickly lowered her hand from the jaw, which was turning a deep blue.

For a little while he looked like a small boy just about to cry. "I'm sorry; I never hit a girl before in my life."

"It's all right," Pat said, her words a little mushed up. It hurt to talk.

The boy looked down again, speaking softly so they had to strain forward to hear him.

"I guess you noticed that sometimes my mother acts like she isn't here. She's nervous and she really needs me to look after her. But how can I when she dumped me on my aunt?"

"Son," Mr. Haley said kindly, "will you let me talk to your mother? I honestly think that if I told her you did all those things just so that you and she could live together away from here, she'd understand."

Dan shrugged, still staring at his feet.

"I don't have much hope. I begged and begged for her not to send me away right after dad died. Not once did she even come to see me."

"It would have hurt her too much to see you," Mrs. Haley said. "Please let Mr. Haley go to see her tomorrow. . . . My!" she broke off, looking outside. "It's tomorrow now. Bob, why don't you go up there. We'll find some dry clothes of Kurt's; and Granny and I will fix us all a good, hot breakfast." She smiled at Dan. "And no one turns down my muffins."

Dan looked at her in surprise. "You'd feed me even after all I've done?"

"Well, we don't exactly approve of using hatchets on boats and furniture, but that's something you and your mother can settle. And I'm sure you will."

Kurt dug in a drawer and got out clothes to give Dan.

"Come, let's get breakfast. Right, Granny? And you come with us, Pat. I'll put ice on that jaw."

Later Mrs. Sweeny came down and went into the cottage where Dan waited. Kurt crossed over to Pat, who sat with a clean rag and ice held to her jaw.

"That sure was a spunky thing for you to do, Pat. There aren't many girls would do a thing that brave."

"There aren't many girls can play short-stop like I can either."

He nodded, "You're a whale of a shortstop, and you don't make errors. We fired Fat. Want a job?"